Text and illustr

Monica Carr

Witches Handbook

CUENTO
DE LUZ

When we arrived, our aunt was waiting for us at the front door. She greeted us with a big smile and motioned for us to enter her gloomy mansion as in a thin, quavering voice she said, "Come in, dear niece and nephew. There's not much time left and I need to share with you a secret which must never be lost." She paused and added in a plaintive voice, "I fear that everything will be forgotten..."

"Dear children, I'm not going to beat around the bush, as we don't have much time. I have every reason to suspect that I am the last witch left in the world," she said as a tear slid down her cheek.

"I must tell you some of the secrets of the lives of the hundreds of witches like me who have lived throughout history. Everything is in this book, but legend has it that these pages will disappear when the last witch dies. And I am on the verge of moving on to a better life. That is why I must tell you everything, so that none of it will be forgotten. For although we witches are bad—far be it from me to deny it—most of us ended up this way out of loneliness and sorrow... Just one kiss would have done us so much good... But there's no time. I will begin."

Witches handbook

What is a witch or a warlock?

Witches and warlocks are crafty, eccentric, wicked and disorganized, although they are also very knowledgeable about any sort of business that is on the shady side. They are people with very, and I mean very, small hearts—so small that they do not know how to love. That is why they cannot give anyone a kiss, they cannot hug, and they do not know how to take pleasure in the happiness of others.

A witch cannot stand kisses or hugs. And a warlock absolutely hates seeing people smile.

It enrages them to know that people love each other. That is why they live alone and far away from the rest of humanity. But above all, witches and warlocks have extraordinary powers which they use only to make mischief.

Is she a witch?
She does not look like one.

It is usually easy to recognize a witch, as she will have an unmistakably outlandish style, but sometimes they try to trick us by adopting an innocent appearance.

Do not let them fool you!

If you are not sure, all you have to do is approach her affectionately, acting ready to cover her with kisses. If she runs away, her face screwed up in disgust, you can be certain:

SHE IS A WITCH!

The geography of witches

Hundreds of witches and warlocks once inhabited our planet from north to south and east to west. Not one single continent escaped the fear of their presence somewhere in its lands. Some achieved fame and were known by all. Others, however, gave free rein to their mischief in the most complete anonymity.

Ha, hee, hi, hoo, hu! Hee, hee, ha!
(laughter of witches and warlocks)

Famous witches and warlocks

Many witches grew very famous and their evil deeds were immortalized in well-known tales. Almost all of them were dissatisfied, bitter, selfish and extremely envious women. Women who, protective of their solitude, played all manner of tricks on others to make sure nobody came close to them. Or they were so eager for power that they would get rid of anyone who got in the way of their quest for glory. There were also male wizards, although not very many, and because they had been born men, they had easier access to what the witches longed for: Power.

The Witch from Snow White

She was a great horticulturist and grew the most extraordinary apples on the continent. Those who managed to survive the first bite of her apples (Snow White among them) say that they have never tasted a more exquisite morsel. Her friendship with a mirror made her bitter. As vain as the vainest among them, she could not stand the idea of any woman being more beautiful. Gossip has it that she put an end to as many beautiful ladies as the number of pounds of apples her fruit trees produced. A lover of disguises and enemy of men of diminutive stature, she spent her final years making compote (apple, of course).

The Witch from Sleeping Beauty

This witch's beauty was comparable only to her wickedness. She loved poppies and used them to make anyone who annoyed her or whom she simply did not like fall asleep for years. At the height of her powers, she caused Princess Aurora (aka Sleeping Beauty) and the 300 inhabitants of the castle to sleep for 100 years. When the parents of the victim asked the witch why she had done it, she answered coldly: "I was not invited to the princess's christening." This witch loved scarves and always traveled with a distaff.

The Witch from Hansel and Gretel

Famous for making the best sweets anybody had ever tasted, this witch lived in a magical castle made of chocolate and caramel. The lost boys and girls who stumbled across this paradise (lollipop trees, grass made of cotton candy, lakes of chocolate...) would start to eat and eat, and then they would eat some more. They ate so much that in the end they could not move, no matter what happened... It is probably best if I do not tell you the rest! It is most unpleasant!

Merlin

Merlin was not exactly a warlock, but rather a magician. However, he is included in the *Witches Handbook* because the witches were all secretly in love with him.

Merlin knew about the essence of all things: He knew the secrets of the sun, of the moon, of the stars in the sky. He knew how to read the future in the magical images of the clouds. He knew the mysteries of the sea... Witches and monsters admired him, for he was an exceptional man.

He was, to be sure, a little given to meddling in the love lives of others, and anyone who doubts this should go ask poor King Arthur! It is said that he lived out his final days imprisoned in a tree as punishment for falling in love with someone he should not have.

Baba Yaga

Baba Yaga was the forerunner of modern architects. Her hut stood on chicken legs and she was constantly refurbishing it: a little bit bigger one day, a little bit smaller the next... Baba Yaga was a real show-off: she loved flying around in a mortar, using her broom to steer.

The Witches from Macbeth

Also known as the "Weird Sisters." Obsessed with the future, they spent their days making prophecies: whether this or that would occur, what things you will or will not do, if what is written will happen to you, and what is beyond... They made the lives of those around them completely crazy!

Unknown witches and warlocks

They may be unknown, but that does not mean they were any less wicked than those who saw their life stories put down in print. Why did they never feature in a fairy tale? Why did they not become famous? Very simple: because in this life, it is not always the best (in this case, the most wicked) who achieve fame.

Witchy San

One of the evil habits of this Japanese witch was to sneak up behind someone taking an exam and when he was about to choose the correct answer, she would whisper in his ear: "A is C and B is D, A is C and B is D," while laughing and chanting, "Ha ha ha, Japanese, ha ha ha, Japanese!" She had a black belt in all the martial arts and owned the loveliest kimonos. She was also a great expert in the ancient art of tea.

Hallowina

An incredible party animal. Considered an excellent hostess, she threw successful parties for guests from both near (the living) and far (the spirits). Everyone got along wonderfully, sharing sandwiches and conversation. Her gatherings were the forerunners of the famous Halloween festival celebrated every year on the night of October 31st.

Malodorous Love

This witch prepared the best potions for causing bad breath, excessive perspiration, extreme nasal congestion, bad digestion and embarrassing stomach noises. Her contemporaries feared her because her spells destroyed many a beautiful love story.

Suffice it to say that Malodorous Love brought romanticism to its knees.

The Meddler

Wicked, wicked, super wicked.
Unpleasant, unpleasant, super
unpleasant. A decrepit, rude,
loudmouthed liar, fool, gossip
and nitpicker. As ugly as could
be. Inveterate egocentric.
In short, The Meddler was
number one in the ranks of the
warlocks.
Legend has it that nobody ever
loved him. Not even the witches
could stand to be around him
for more than ten minutes.

Witch Dimwit

Dimwit, despite her dazed expression,
sowed terror throughout the local
villages. She was truly stupid, and
there is nothing worse than giving
powers to a silly fool because they
do everything "willy-nilly." Dimwit did
not think things through: one moment
she would be turning a prince into a
frog and the next taking away a lady's
voice. As a curiosity, we might add
that she always traveled on a mop
rather than a broom.

Dolores Batunga-tunga

This African witch was famous for her dances. Their pure beauty and power hypnotized anyone who saw them, leaving them at her mercy.

She had a strong and passionate personality and was a great visionary and expert in evil concoctions and potions. Her terrible spells were capable of controlling the skies, and with them the clouds, and with the clouds, the water.

Serafina the Terrible

A Spanish witch. Her power lay in controlling the forces of evil by directing animals using strange noises such as:
YEEEAH! TUUUURRI!
CROAK-CROAK!
and HI-HAAA-HI-HAAAAA!
Serafina communicated with animals with great ease and joy. No human was ever able to understand a single word that came out of her mouth. Down-to-earth, pigheaded and fond of singing, she would roam the forest, completely at ease, sowing catastrophes like swarms of rats or cockroaches.

Bad Temper Warlock

Another warlock, and you may have noted that we have seen only two. The thing is, there were not that many warlocks, but they were so wicked that each one was worth one hundred witches. Devilishly bad-tempered. With virtually no provocation, Bad Luck would find a reason to get into a broom fight with anyone who crossed his path.

Doña Amarga

That is me. A lovely old lady, a sweet woman with a melodious voice who sings charming songs that make you sigh. And when you have just begun to trust me...

I TURN INTO A BAD
WITCH! HA, HA, HA!
EVIL BAD!
HEE, HA, HOO!
I'LL GOBBLE YOU UP,
AS EASY AS YOU PLEASE!
HEE, HA, HOO!

When were there more witches?

Without a doubt, in the Middle Ages. But during that period, you would do better to act very normal, because if your tastes ran to anything a little out of the ordinary, you would quickly be branded a wanton witch. Do you think you can find the real witches in this old drawing? If you have been paying careful attention to this guide, you are sure to spot them!

The broom: mode of transportation

Brooms in their many different varieties have always carried witches from one place to another.

Some examples of brooms

6 feet 2 inches

In order to fly properly, it is important for the broom and witch to be the same height. The size of the broom has nothing to do with the speed achieved. The broom is a maneuverable, quick, cool and eco-friendly mode of transportation. It offers a perfect bird's-eye view and the broom's shape makes it easy to fly between trees in the forest.

(There is always someone who prefers new technology.)

Flying styles

Both witches and warlocks are experts in the art of broom flying and they do so with style.
Here are a few examples:

1. Meditation Style
2. Perfect Balance Style
3. Backwards Style
4. I'm Falling Style
5. Aggressive Style
6. Standard Style
7. Night Owl Style

Witches and animals

As we have already pointed out, witches hate kissing and cuddling. If they ever say anything even a little nice, they are talking to their animals. The animals that accompany witches on their adventures are normally unpleasant, disagreeable and somewhat repulsive. They act as companions or as basic ingredients in the witches' potions.

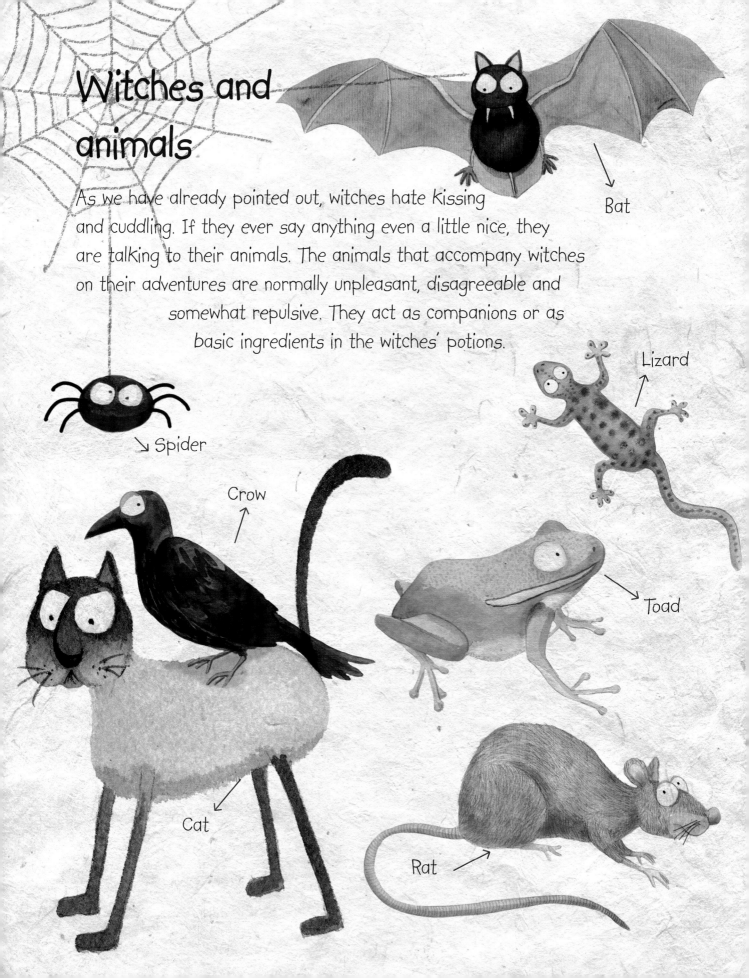

Bat

Lizard

↘ Spider

Crow

Toad

Cat

Rat

Potions and spells

If there is anything witches were known for, it was being connoisseurs of the evil effects that can be achieved by combining herbs, plants and small animals. By mixing them together in a cauldron over low heat and chanting strange and foul words, they were able to create the most evil potions in the whole wide world. With these potions they could do whatever they wanted: turn a prince into a frog, put a young girl to sleep for years, make a wolf able to talk so that he could pass for an old lady, call up storms that would cause the most terrible captain to wreck, break up any number of romances...

It is extremely difficult to find an antidote to these spells and enchantments. There is only one cure for most of them. Do you know what it is? That's right! A kiss. A marvelous kiss saved Snow White, Sleeping Beauty and hundreds of princes that had been turned into amphibians. A kiss can cure almost anything!

Halloween and the witches' sabbat

Witches love to have a good time. That is why whenever they can, they organize gatherings to sing and dance in the light of the moon.

The sabbat gatherings held by Spanish witches were famous. In addition to having a high old time, they were always accompanied by a black kid goat, an essential element at these meetings. In fact, the witches' festival par excellence is Halloween, which is celebrated on the night of October 31st. Guests at this party include spirits, ghosts, monsters (the ugly kind) and, of course, all the witches. It is great fun. If you dare to join in, you too are invited.

Your authors urge you most earnestly to attend!

Aunt Amarga was still reading us *Witches Handbook* when she suddenly sneezed. We looked at her and saw that she had turned into a frog.

"Aunt Amarga, is that you? What happened?" we asked.

But the frog wearing braids and dressed in our aunt's clothing just hopped into Leo's hands, gazed happily at us and immediately hopped right out the window. When she got to the lake, she leaped onto a lily pad and lay down in the sun as happy as you please.

"I think Aunt Amarga has moved on to a better life," Leo said.

"So it would seem... And now that Aunt Amarga is gone, witches no longer exist. She was the last one," I answered sadly.

But then I realized that *Witches Handbook* was still sitting there.

It hadn't disappeared. That meant
that...
Yes! I was sure of it!
There was still a witch hiding
away in a forest somewhere!

Witches Handbook

Text & Illustrations© 2011 Monica Carretero
This edition © 2011 Cuento de Luz SL
Calle Claveles 10 | Urb Monteclaro | Pozuelo de Alarcón
28223 Madrid | Spain | www.cuentodeluz.com

Original title in Spanish: Manual de Brujas
Translated into English by Cálamo & Cran (Nedra Rivera Huntington)

ISBN: 9788415241065

Printed by Shanghai Chenxi Printing Co., Ltd. in PRC,
September 2011, print number 1227-5

FSC
www.fsc.org
MIX
Paper from
responsible sources
FSC® C007923